A Bead of Amber on Her Tongue

A Bead of Amber on Her Tongue
Jennifer Pullen

OMNIDAWN PUBLISHING
OAKLAND, CALIFORNIA
2019

Cover art by Stephanie Law
"Awakened," watercolor. www.shadowscapes.com

Cover set in Adobe Garamond Pro
Interior set in Gramond 3 LT Std and Adobe Garmond Pro
Cover and Interior design by Trisha Peck

Printed in the United States
by Books International, Dulles, Virginia
On 55# Glatfelter B19 Antique
Acid Free Archival Quality Recycled Paper

Library of Congress Cataloging-in-Publication Data

Names: Pullen, Jennifer, 1986- author.
Title: A bead of amber on her tongue / Jennifer Pullen.
Description: Oakland, California : Omnidawn Publishing, 2019.
Identifiers: LCCN 2018040202 | ISBN 9781632430694 (pbk. : alk.   paper)
Subjects: LCSH: Aphrodite (Greek deity)--Fiction. | Helen, of Troy,
    Queen of Sparta--Fiction.
Classification: LCC PS3616.U458 A6 2019 | DDC 813/.6--dc23
LC record available at https://lccn.loc.gov/2018040202

Published by Omnidawn Publishing, Oakland, California
www.omnidawn.com (510) 237-5472 (800) 792-4957
10 9 8 7 6 5 4 3 2 1
ISBN: 978-1-63243-069-4

Acknowledgments

To my many advisers, but especially Joan, thank you. Extra thanks to my parents who never once suggested that I should try to be anything other than writer, and who let me have a Greek mythology coloring book at an oddly young age. Last, but most definitely not least, thank you to my husband, my self-described "biggest fan," for all his support.

Table of Contents

Aphrodite Plays the Shell Game

I

Aphrodite sits on the floor of Zeus's throne room, her legs crossed, the marble floor cool against her legs. She can feel the disapproving glance of Hera against her back, but she doesn't care. She has no interest in the proceedings. The activities of minor gods coming to petition her father, as far as she's concerned, are nothing but simple routine enactments. Water nymphs arguing, saying: she usurped my stream, no, she did, no, she did. Household gods complaining that they are no longer being worshipped properly, that sort of thing. She stacks carved bone dice on top of each other, lowering each one gently on top of the next, conscious also of the eyes of her lover Ares lingering on her game.

He strolls over, his leather armor creaking, and crouches on the floor next to her, and asks if he can play. She grins up at him, tells him no, she prefers to play alone. He raises one dark eyebrow.

"I find that hard to believe," he says.

She twirls a die between her fingertips and gestures towards the stack of wooden cups in the corner. Ares hands them to her, and she puts them flat on the marble floor, and holds up the die again.

"Watch my hands," she says.

She hears the tap of the house steward's staff calling the next petitioner forward. Feet shuffle. She glances over her shoulder, sees a group of men carrying a large and heavy object draped in linen. Probably yet another gift to curry favor with Hera. She turns away. She hears a murmur of voices, but blocks them out, and shakes her head as Ares starts to turn around to look. She tells him again to watch. She places the die under one of the cups. She asks him if he saw where she put it. He nods. She moves the cups around and they make soft rubbing sounds on the marble, which remind her of the sea rolling back the tide, but at a whisper.

She's about to ask Ares if he can find the die, when a voice breaks the ceremonial hush. Someone drops a bronze goblet in a clatter to the ground.

"What have you done, cinder-dwarf? I can't get up."

Aphrodite turns and sees Hera, sitting on a new golden throne, kicking and straining, pushing so hard her hands make dents in the metal, but unable to get up. Hephaestus stands in front of the throne, his feet set wide despite his shriveled leg, his hands held at his sides. Aphrodite can see his arms trembling from her place across the room.

"I've simply made you a very comfortable throne," he says.

"Filth," says Hera. She's gritting her teeth and her eyes do not promise pleasure to the man standing before her.

Aphrodite watches, rapt. When Ares tries to speak she shushes him, squeezing his thigh hard. Hera has never liked her, always hated her for being one more product of Zeus's infidelities. Once, when she was a child, Hera tried to drown her, dropping her into a well. But a water sprite that lived in the well kept her from sinking. Another time, many other times, Hera slapped her, especially as she grew more beautiful, as her power manifested. So, she can't help but enjoy seeing the proud goddess discomfited. She almost begins to like Hephaestus in that moment, odd, twisted god of smiths that he is.

Zeus stands up and grasps his wife's shoulders. He pulls, his muscles straining. Hera screeches and tells him to stop. He's hurting her. Aphrodite laughs, and her voice echoes in the room. Hera glares at her. Zeus turns on Hephaestus.

"You have power over all metal, so set your queen free, now." Thunder growls outside.

Hephaestus shrugs. "As you wish, but grant me one boon."

"What do you want, wily little man?"

Hephaestus doesn't acknowledge the insult. Aphrodite wonders what he wants, what could have made him play this prank, despite the fact that being a trickster has never been his nature. Ares leans over, breathes in her ear, says he thinks Hephaestus may have gotten too hot over his forge, and boiled his brains. She shushes him again. She needs to hear. She can feel that this concerns her, feel the threads of the Fates thrum.

"Let me marry your daughter."

"Which one? I have many."

"The only one that matters. Aphrodite."

Aphrodite stands up, the cups spilling away from her feet, the dice tower demolished. Ares tries to grab at her hand, but she shakes him off, no time for love right now.

"You are mad," she says.

"You must be mad," Zeus says.

"I must be." Hephaestus nods. But he doesn't take back his demand.

Zeus looks at Hera and she looks right back at him and Aphrodite can see history flow between them and knows she's lost.

"Very well," Zeus says.

Hephaestus makes a motion with his hand, and Hera jumps up from the throne, pushes it over with one smooth motion. She tells them to take it away.

Ares stands, grasps her shoulder, and says they must run.

She thinks about shrugging off his hand, but then decides against it, knows that this may be the last time he can touch her like this, in public.

"What would be the point?" she asks.

Ares looks down at the scattered cups. He points to one of them, tipped on its side.

"The die was under that one," he says. Then he lets go of her and strides out of the room. She watches him go, his broad back, his scarred arms, and doesn't blame him for not wanting to see whatever is about to happen next. She looks back at the cups.

"Not that one," she murmurs.

Aphrodite's room, all white linen and gleaming cedar wood, overlooking the sea, used to please her, but now she hates the whole place, hates the bevy of maids running around the room, gathering her wedding attire. Aphrodite knows she should never have laughed when Hera sat down on the golden throne and then couldn't get up. She should never have chuckled at the sight of her stepmother straining and failing to extract herself from a mere chair. That chuckle is probably part of why she has to sit still, has to let maids weave honeysuckle and apple blossoms into her hair, let them rub her body with perfumed oil, has to let them prepare her to be married. Her laughter, and Hephaestus's absurd demand, Hera's hatred for her, and Zeus's weakness, all have brought her to this pass. Zeus tends to do what his wife tells him to do, which Aphrodite assumes is some misplaced effort on his part to make Hera forgive or approve his many liaisons with other women, both mortal and immortal. One of the maids leans over and kisses her cheek. Aphrodite looks up, startled. The girl has plump pink cheeks and soft blonde curls. The girl blushes under her examination.

"I'm getting married soon too," she says, and scurries out of the room. One of the naiads among the ladies floats over, ivy growing in her hair.

"They think your touch on your wedding day will make them fertile," she says.

"Not when I feel this way," Aphrodite says.

But the naiad has already left, drifting toward the window, called by the breeze. Aphrodite envies her. Another maid comes over, starts rubbing rose scented cream over her arms and legs, and she tries not to feel it, tries to drift away in her mind.

She waits until the maids have finished adorning her and left the room, secure in the perception that they've done as ordered. As soon as they disappear, she strips the flowers from her hair and changes out of her red silk gown to one of plain pale cotton. Zeus can force her to marry but she won't let him have her painted into a façade of celebration.

The sound of horns echoes through her room and the wind blows her curtains. She considers rending her hair and scratching her face in mourning like the humans do—but deems it too dramatic. She can't really envision harming herself. She also toys with climbing out of her window and walking barefoot across the grass and leaving Olympus, hiding in some shepherd's hut and having lots of half mortal babies. But of course, that wouldn't work, because her father, being Zeus, would find her. She might have time to find a young shepherd with winsome eyes, but definitely no time to make babies. Besides, she doesn't want to marry a shepherd any more than she wants to marry Hephaestus. So she settles for her small, attire-shaped rebellion, and goes into the hall where a cluster of her maids and forest nymphs wait to escort her.

The nymphs, at least, look sympathetic. They curse men for looking at them without permission, let alone for something like this. One of the maids holds out a circlet of finely worked gold crusted with emeralds. They beg her to wear it. They say her husband-to-be made it just for her. She dashes the circlet to the floor and pushes through the crowd of women.

At the end of the hall is a courtyard, and she can see Ares standing there, framed by the doorway, so tall that he blocks her sight of who her father intends her to marry. She wishes she had rent her hair after all. As she passes him she brushes against his side, tries to catch his scent of sweat, horses, and wine. He doesn't ask her to run again, but she knows he wants to. She knows his weakness for any futile endeavor. She steps into the light and sees Hephaestus, waiting, dressed in red, grinning as though he's won a prize. He holds an arm out to her. She takes it, but she can't feel the press of his flesh against hers. She feels as if she's being escorted by a phantom, or perhaps she's the one growing insubstantial. Hephaestus tries to talk to her, but she's tumbling around in her own thoughts and can't hear him.

She has never liked Hephaestus. When they were children he used to throw mud at her. He hated her for beating him in the games of tag among the divine children. It wasn't her fault that his leg was deformed and his mother found him revolting. It wasn't her fault that everyone was always stroking her cheek and talking about what a beautiful child she was. She didn't choose her fate any more than he did. But he was always around, always watching her, always glowering under his dark brows. She did her best to ignore him. Once he gave her a bracelet of finely braided bronze. It was beautiful. She's not surprised he turned out to be the god of the forges. He was mostly sullen and morose, not cruel, at least as far as she remembers. But that doesn't mean she's happy about being on his arm, that her father is making her marry him, just because he was able to get Hera off the idiotic magic throne that he built as a trap in the first place. As far as Aphrodite is concerned, Hera should have just stayed there; it would have served her right for being foolish enough to fall for such a trick. Didn't the Trojan War teach anybody anything?

"We're here," Hephaestus says. He squeezes her arm harder, and she startles, realizes that they are standing under a bronzed dome with white pillars. She just stands there and lets her father bind her and her husband's wrists together with silken cords. She feels herself crying and wishes that tears could make her ugly. When Zeus declares them married Hephaestus leans forward and whispers that he did it all for her, so that her father would allow the marriage. He continues to whisper about how she was always so kind to him, how she never mocked him for being ugly, and how, one time, she brought him an apple. She takes back all of her previous assessments. He never used to be cruel, but now he acts both cruel and delusional, mistaking childhood pity for everlasting love.

She stares over his shoulder at her lover, at his dark eyes and his callused hands. His temples look tight from the clenching of his jaw. She wants to smooth away his distress. She knows in that moment that her father as the king of the gods can make her marry whomever he pleases, but he can't keep her from taking after him, from giving her body to whomever she wants. He can't make her be faithful. Hephaestus, well, he will get what he won—an unwilling wife.

II

Aphrodite likes to keep secrets. She hasn't told anyone that she leaves Olympus to swim naked in the ocean at night. Sometimes sailors see her and think she's a Nereid, or a mermaid. Once a young fisherman thought she was a local maiden drowning and tried to rescue her. He threw her a rope and cried for her to catch it. She grabbed the rope and loved the roughness of it under her fingers, so different from her own skin. When he pulled her to the edge of his boat she could see his dark curls and teenage pimples. He stared at her neck and her breasts and forgot to speak. She laughed, blew him a kiss and allowed herself to dissolve into the sea foam which her father Zeus sometimes says she was born from. The sea could never harm her, so that particular secret stays small, sweet, and safe, like a bead of amber to roll around on her tongue.

Tonight, she sits on the beach and makes sand palaces. She imagines herself in her own palace, one in which she isn't one more product of Zeus's adulterous affairs, a palace where Hera, her stepmother, would be obliged to be polite to her because one must always be polite to one's hosts. As she sits there, sand between her toes and her wet hair clinging to her back and waist, she hears footsteps and the clink of armor. She turns and sees Ares, his sword still wet with blood in his hand, but his breastplate unscarred by blows.

"A great warrior would know to clean his sword," she says, and goes back to building her castles, shaping the domes and the courtyards with care. She can feel his eyes on her body, and she revels in her power. Her father may be able to throw lighting and her step-mother bring life to the earth, but she can make anyone long for her touch, even the god of war. Then the tip of his sword touches the back of her neck. He says that most people would be far too afraid to insult his skill as a warrior. She can smell his sweat, the blood on the sword, and feel the rumble of his voice. His voice is like a herd of horses running from a storm. She turns her head to look at him and the point of the sword falls away.

"I'm afraid I don't have any wine to offer you, my castle is so new," she says and gestures towards her miniature sandy fortress.

He laughs, holds out his hand, and pulls her to her feet. He asks if her father knows where she is.

"My father knows very little," she says.

III

Ares feels useless in her presence. He knows many things, the exact way to pound a shield so it sounds like thunder, or how to always find a man's heart with the tip of a sword. He can feel the blood of men like a pulse in his own divine flesh. He's sent many on their journey across the river Styx. He doesn't feel bad about it either. As the god of war, he is what he is. He can no more stop fighting than Hades can learn to plant roses. Sometimes, after a battle, he meets Hades in the underworld for a skin's worth of wine. They sit in silence and think about what to do with gentle women. Hades moans about Persephone's moods, and Ares nods in sympathy.

Last week she hid his sword and wouldn't say where it was until he found her secret flaw. He read the story of her body like a scroll rolled across her skin. The skin on the underside of her arms was like a shell, her hair made of sun, her lips of nectar. He couldn't detect a single blemish. She finally showed him the tiny freckle between her two littlest toes.

He knows it's dangerous to adore the goddess of love and beauty; he can't compel her to do anything, let alone love him only and always. He should be ashamed of the way he ignores the calls to battle, the ram's horns being blown, the sharpening of weapons. He's supposed to be lending courage to men at war, but he tells himself that humans are good enough at killing each other without his help. Besides, she's been busy making up stories for his each and every scar. He can worry later about battles and what her father will say if he finds out, after she finishes making him lick mead out of her navel.

IV

Aphrodite never lets Hephaestus touch her. She won't even let him sleep in their bed. She shuts the door in his face and knows he doesn't have the courage to break it down. He tells her that he can shape swords with his hands and hammer metal as hot as the sun, so he can certainly break down her door. She tells him to go ahead, to prove he's a brute. He never does.

She lets the linen sheets cool her flesh and then dreams of her lover, of their meetings on the beach, of the sea songs and war chants he recites to her. The words don't matter, only the way his chest vibrates against her ear. He can lay waste to entire armies. He consorts with Hades, but he touches her as though she were a blossom. He never asks about her husband, about that one time with Hermes, or the way the fishermen stare at her naked body in the sea. He understands that weights, ropes or demands make her feel sick and sallow. He would never try to hold her, to bind her. That's why she stays with him, that why it's been ages since she touched another. That's why she never takes pity on Hephaestus even though he weeps, even though he stares at the children of other gods and carves little wooden chariots.

She has named the secret in her womb Harmonia.

V

When she draws his head down to her stomach and begs him to listen, he feels the same way he always does before a battle. The tiny heart beat makes him feel mortal and weak. How can he raise a daughter when his lover is the wife of another? He considers killing Hephaestus, half man that he is, even though there would be no honor in it. She tells him that he can't kill her husband or Zeus will try to kill him, and then there would be war among the immortals…and who wants that? He mutters that she seems to forget what exactly he's god of—he's always up for a good war. Ares is only partially jesting, the idea of spreading blood over the world like olive oil on bread sounds rather appealing at the moment. He hates the fact that he has no control, that the strength in his arms is as useless as an eggshell.

"My sword is getting dull," he says and rests his head in his hands, his dark hair falling over his face in knots. She stops lolling on the sand and crawls over to him. Through his hair he can see grains of sand sticking to her knees and thighs. She grasps between his legs.

"Is it?" she asks.

He catches both her wrists and stands, drawing her upward, and wraps his arms around her to keep her still. Her skin feels hot. "You will not distract me," he says. She bites his shoulder and he understands she can't help her nature any more than he can help his; the Fates wove them both. She says that she is going to have to sleep with Hephaestus to make him think the child is his. He holds her tighter and wonders why even gods have these problems. Such worries should belong to fishermen and farmers. He wonders why the idea of Aphrodite's husband raising the child, braiding her hair and teaching her to read, feels worse than the idea of Aphrodite sleeping with the cripple.

"Just this once," he says.

Even as the words leave his mouth he knows that nothing will stop Hephaestus from finding out eventually. Eternity unspools with plenty of time to uncover an affair. If he were Hephaestus, if he were the type of man who needed to trap a wife, to devise clever schemes for the simplest situations, then he would probably be biding his time and plotting not only to catch Aphrodite being unfaithful, but to humiliate her too.

VI

Aphrodite doesn't need to plan the day she sleeps with Hephaestus, because the situation warrants capitulation on her part, not seduction, but she does it anyway. She dabs oil of jasmine on her wrists and combs her golden curls until they float around her like an aura. She wraps herself in nearly sheer blue silk which can be undone with the twist of an ivory pin. She removes all her jewelry, refusing to have any metal, any of his elements, around her. She presses her hands to her stomach and imagines another life, one where being a goddess could save her from being a pawn in games of power, one where she and Ares go live on a ship with purple sails and travel the world together. Ares would teach her daughter to hold a sword and shoot a bow. She'd teach her daughter how to play the lute and the power of a glance over a bare shoulder to arouse anyone. Their daughter would be a warrior beauty, strong. No one would force her to do anything ever. Unfortunately, making dreams come alive is not one of Aphrodite's powers.

Hephaestus can't come home without her knowing; he'll smell like smoke and sulfur from the forges until he takes a bath. Sitting on the edge of her bed, perched like a falcon in jesses, she waits. Mechanically she eats a bowl of grapes and drinks glass after glass of wine. She wishes she was mortal just so she could pray to Dionysus to make the wine work quick, to take her senses so she won't have to feel what she's about to do. She doesn't want to touch her husband; it makes her feel like her stomach houses a nest of ants, constantly crawling. It isn't his ugliness she hates. As the goddess of beauty she knows that everything is beautiful if looked at in the right way, what she hates is the fact that he never asked what she wanted, he never courted her; he used her father to force her into this situation. It makes her feel like an object, like a cup or a shield won in battle, valuable but unfeeling. Being forced into marriage feels representative of all the awful things the male gods do, descending on women and taking their bodies without one word. Zeus raping Leda is just one example among many. She hears the door open; she smells the detritus of fire and molten metal and knows Hephaestus is home.

Taking another deep swallow of wine she sets the cup down on the floor and tips it over. A little wine dribbles on the floor. Aphrodite rumples the covers of the bed and lies down on her side making sure her hair falls across her cheek and her breasts—pseudo disarray. To make the picture complete she rumples her dress so it rides up on one side, revealing one long pale leg. She hears Hephaestus come into the room. He whispers her name once. She doesn't respond, controlling her breathing in a façade of sleep. He says her name louder. She shifts and murmurs as though moderately disturbed and then turns her head so as to expose the line of her throat. He approaches the bed and puts the wine glass upright. Its base clinks against the marble floor. The bed shifts as he sits on the edge. He runs one finger over the bottom of her foot and then encircles her ankle. His hands are rough and callused, and feel too much like the hands of her lover for comfort; there is surprisingly little difference between a callus from swinging a hammer or a sword. He bends and places a kiss on her ankle.

"I'm sorry," he says.

She opens her eyes slowly and looks at him. The sleepy eyes and bleariness are pretense but real confusion riots within her. His gentleness and his words, spoken when he thought she couldn't hear, make her world so much more complicated. He crawls up onto the bed, his crippled leg temporarily invisible. He brushes a thumb across the corner of her mouth, wiping at a spot of dried wine.

"Are you all right?" he asks.

"No," she says.

"Did you drink too much?"

"Yes."

He kisses her and she lets him. He runs his hands through her hair and nuzzles between her breasts and she lets him. She can't manage more than passivity. A keening wail fills her head. She wonders what happens to a goddess who acts against her nature. At the end she feels dampness on her neck, and she realizes that he's crying. She lets him rest his head on her breasts and she strokes his hair which is straight and surprisingly soft. This moment will have to be another secret.

VII

Aphrodite's waist doesn't grow thick and clumsy, but rather round and fecund. Ares can't get enough of kneeling on the sand and telling stories to the general vicinity of her navel. He tells of his feats of daring, hoping that somehow the little god-child will hear and remember who her real father is. Hephaestus just presses his hands on either side of her stomach and closes his eyes, as though he can feel the movements of the infant through her skin. He seems to think that the night Aphrodite let him make love to her and then fall asleep next to her means that she loves him now and that everything is just the way he always wanted it to be. He keeps bringing her little shiny pebbles, or bits of metal he's worked into clever shapes. She doesn't know how to dissuade him without making him suspicious, so she lets him think what he wants. Even though she doesn't encourage him, act affectionate, or let him into her bed again, she feels guilty, like the time as a child she squished a butterfly because Hera said it was more beautiful than she was.

Ares starts to get jealous. He keeps asking why she lets Hephaestus hold her hand in public and drink from her cup at feasts. She explains that she doesn't want their sacrifice, the one time she let her husband touch her, to be for nothing. What would the point be if he figures out that the child isn't his? But Ares broods and throws rocks into the sea and looks dissatisfied. He turns to her and takes her hand, massaging her palm.

"If you really love me, if you haven't started to like him, take me to your house, let me touch you in your bed, not here on the sand, in secret," he says.

She agrees, because she can see the bruise in his eyes. Hephaestus is working on a big project anyway, some sort of golden chariot. He won't be home until late, so she takes Ares to the house. On the bed, its huge cedar frame and canopy above and around them instead of the stars, Ares places kisses on each of her palms, and then her feet, evoking each of the four winds on the four corners of her flesh; Boreas, Notos, Eurus, and Zephyrus. She asks him why.

"So you don't blow away," he says.

His words make her nervous, like they portend a tragedy, but eventually she loses herself in his skin on her skin, on his whispered words in her ear. She closes her eyes to better focus on the feel of body against body, and she can't help but think that the rhythms of love are like waves, and she wonders what it would be like to join with the god of the sea. She doesn't know why she opens her eyes, just for a second, but when she does she sees Hephaestus standing in the doorway, metal gleaming in his hands. He releases a golden net, flinging it over their conjoined bodies. It must hurt, because Ares roars in pain and thrashes around, but Aphrodite just holds still, because gold obeys the god of smiths; just like when he forged Hera's golden throne into a trap, only he can release them.

"Maybe you'll tire of each other now," Hephaestus says and then turns and walks away.

Ares curses, swears revenge, and tries to get her to discuss battle plans, but she just makes soothing noises and presses her hand to his cheek. She'll never tell Ares that Hephaestus looked at her, held her eyes, that there was a second when she could have cried out, when Ares could have leapt up and dashed the net to the ground, if only she'd said something, but she didn't. When she saw the net in her husband's hands she could almost hear the threads woven by the Fates thrum, and she knew that he needed to throw that net, and that some part of her felt she deserved it. Not for giving her body and her heart to Ares, but for letting Hephaestus be-lieve that she loved him, for granting him a taste of tenderness and then taking it away, her hands in his hair, his head on her breasts.

Coral Covered Her Bones

After she gets out of the bath Helen makes a tiny cut on her upper thigh with her knife and watches the blood rise to the surface. The red against her pale flesh makes her feel like vomiting and laughing at the same time. She thinks the blood must want to get out because it rushes so quickly out of her body. She holds a little cloth to her leg until it stops bleeding and smiles at the pain. It's not that she enjoys hurting herself, but she wants to see if someone will notice, or admit to noticing. She hopes it will scar. She rinses the blade in the bath water and watches her blood dilute and disappear, brief red swirls. She thinks it might be good to have a secret ugliness.

Helen's maid comes in, tells her it's time to get ready for the banquet. Her maid stares at the knife, at the smear of blood on her thigh. She holds out her hand, and Helen hands her the bloody piece of cloth, even though she knows the girl wanted the knife. She tells her to take it away. The girl takes the bloody cloth and folds it carefully, as if it's a treasure she tucks into the bag at her waist. "There's no magic in my blood, you know," Helen says to the girl. The maid ducks her dark head. Helen thinks her hair looks like a deep pool at night. For a moment she envies such dusky looks, the ability to blend into a crowd, to not be marked everywhere one goes.

"I'm sorry, my lady," the maid says. But she doesn't take the cloth out of her bag. She holds out her hand again and Helen drops the knife in the tub. She knows her displays of power over a servant are silly, pointless. But she doesn't like the way the servants, even this girl, look at her. She's seen them picking her hair out of her brush, and carefully folding away the napkins she spits in. She overheard someone saying something about love charms. It makes her feel as though her whole body is public property.

The girl ignores the knife in the bath and instead picks up a comb of jade and begins yanking it through Helen's hair. Helen doesn't flinch. She remembers once when she sat between her mother's knees as she untangled her long yellow locks. It took what felt like hours and Helen kept trying to squirm away. Her mother held her in a grip like stone and told her the price of beauty was pain, and she might as well get used to it.

"I'll wear red tonight," Helen says.

"Your husband said to dress you in blue for the banquet, to make the visitors think of the sea."

"All the more reason to wear red."

The girl ignores her and keeps combing her hair. Helen doesn't bother to keep arguing, because the maids always listen to Menelaus, not to her. That's why she doesn't care to learn their names anymore. Her first maid, after she got married, was named Esme. Helen used to tell Esme about her childhood in the palace by the river, about how she'd sneak outside and wander through the reeds, looking for the secret nests of swans. Her mother would get angry at her, and then send someone to chase away the birds, but Helen did it anyway. Esme's parents had been fisher-folk, and Esme would tell stories about days out on the sea, hauling fish into the boat, how her hair would get tangled into locks of salt and seaweed. How she'd slice open the bellies of the fish and drop the intestines into the waves. After a long day, she'd go home and bathe in the hot springs by the village, washing fish blood off her face and out from under her nails. At night Esme and her sisters would sleep all together in the same bed—curled in a nest like the hounds in the palace stables.

Every night after Menelaus left Helen, Esme would crawl under the sheets with her and stroke her hair, tell her stories about the sea-maidens who had flippers and loved each other instead of men. One night, Menelaus pinched her arm, hard, told her to stop being so cold. He smiled as he pinched her. He thought he was being funny. He left a bruise. Helen, to spite him, acted as if she didn't feel it. But she knew her attempts at strength and pride were useless because it was all based on the assumption that Menelaus was paying attention.

After he left, she curled up on the bed and found she couldn't cry. It felt as though there were a raisin inside her; a shriveled thing in her chest that wouldn't let her feel. Esme found her like that and kissed the bruise on her arm. She murmured dire words about what she'd like to do to Menelaus, about how, where she came from, men like him were treated like small fish, gutted and used as bait to catch bigger fish, which were at least good to eat. Helen let her go on talking, despite the fact that, truthfully, Menelaus was just dull and unempathetic. He hadn't even realized he'd hurt her. He was always like that. He saw her as a prize not a person, before marrying her the only women he'd had were slaves, and it's not like they ever complained. He didn't even know that there was such a thing as tenderness. Helen knew that other women had husbands who hurt their wives on purpose; her situation could have been much worse. But her knowledge didn't keep her from hating her husband, so she let Esme talk about gutting, about drowning, and she liked what she heard. She let Esme kiss her arm, her face, the nape of her neck. Esme stayed until Helen fell asleep.

Then one day Esme was gone. Menelaus told Helen that it was unseemly for a queen, a demi-goddess at that, to spend so much time talking to a servant. Helen tried to have Esme found. She sent runners to Esme's village, to her parents. But she was gone as though she were words scraped from parchment. Helen thinks

Menelaus probably had her strangled. She's heard rumors he feeds the disobedient to pigs.

So she never asks for the names of the maids anymore.

Now the girl with dark eyes combs out Helen's hair, then presses it dry with yards and yards of white linen. Then she tells Helen to lie down, and Helen lies down on her couch and the girl rubs scented oil into her skin, even between her toes, but she avoids the wound on Helen's upper thigh. Helen looks out the window, and she can see the ocean off in the distance, so blue it almost makes her eyes hurt. She hopes that Menelaus dropped Esme in the sea, that her body sank to the depths and that coral covered her bones, and that now the sea maidens sit on her and sing. She thinks Esme would have preferred that to getting turned into pig shit.

At the banquet Menelaus pulls her to him and kisses her hard on the lips. The men around laugh into their beards. They whistle and hoot. They slap his back. He shouts and proposes a toast to Helen, his wife, the most beautiful woman it the world. They stand, but she stays sitting. Menelaus always starts bragging about her beauty at banquets, about how she doesn't have a mark on her body, how she is like linen and raked sand. He says her breasts are like goblets and, well, certain parts taste of pomegranates. She smiles, because this time he's lying. She does have a mark on her skin. She's felt the wound on her thigh all day as she walked. She presses her hand under the table against the cut. She stares out over the banquet hall, and tries not catch anyone's gaze with her own. She doesn't want to see the hatred in the eyes of the women, or the lust in the eyes of the men. When Menelaus gives these toasts, they all look at her as though they are imagining that they are Menelaus, that they are laying her down on a bed and tasting every inch of her.

Menelaus finishes his speech and then pulls her to her feet and whispers in her ear.

"Turn around, show them I don't lie," he says.

This is the part where she's supposed to act flattered and spin around, flashing a little bit of leg, looking coyly through the fall of her hair braided with pearls and flowers. Menelaus loves to half promise to share her, whisper about her wildness to the other men. Their little Greek kingdom grows rich in trading partners due to such half promises. He never makes good on his half promise, something for which Helen thanks all the gods, but he does make her come and sit with the men, let them talk to her, let them compliment her eyes and her lips, let them kiss her hand and hold the pulse of her wrist against their cheeks. When he lets them do such things, they will promise him anything. *Yes, we'll gladly give you first rights of trade and purchase on our wine, our figs, or our spices from Egypt.* It's like they're hypnotized. Menelaus says she's like a snake from across the sea, the kind with a hood that men teach to dance to the sound of a flute, the kind that can make a man smile as he's bitten. Menelaus shakes her arm, jerks her out of her reverie.

"Come my pretty serpent, turn."

She turns, and as she does so, she catches, without meaning to, the eyes of a young man at the other end of the long table. His hair is dark and curling, like that of most Greeks, but he's beardless and his eyes are as blue as hers. The other men are staring at her breasts, her arms, and her neck. But he looks at her eyes, nods, and then looks down at the ground. Menelaus claps and tells her to spin again. He motions over the older man next to the young one with blue eyes. The older man comes over and takes Helen's hand. Menelaus says something that she doesn't hear and squeezes her breast with an appreciative chortle. She flinches. The older man laughs and drops her hand. He and Menelaus reach for wine glasses and make a toast. She looks over at the young man. He still has his eyes turned toward the ground. She feels like he's given her a gift by not looking, by giving her some privacy in her shame. She slips away from the table, and when Menelaus looks at her she makes a motion at her abdomen, indicating that she has to urinate. He looks away, uninterested now. He's hooked his prey. Today Menelaus is shopping for allies, and the older man is the ambassador for the mighty city of Troy, a valuable catch indeed.

Helen goes out of the front entrance of the banquet hall to stand on a balcony overlooking the sea. She waits for what she knows must be coming. Sure enough, soon she hears the soft slapping sound of sandals on stone, and she turns and sees the young man. He nods and walks to edge of the balcony and stands next to her, staring out at the sea. It's almost dark, and the waves make her think of black sails unfurling in the wind. The young man doesn't speak, doesn't even really acknowledge her presence. She'd expected him to say something, to offer extravagant compliments, to insult Menelaus, call him crude and a brute. She thought he wanted to take to her to bed, and she considers at least letting him kiss her, as a reward for looking away at the banquet and not helping Menelaus display her like a chest full of treasure. But he hasn't even spoken, so she turns and looks at him, admires the long graceful line of his shoulders, muscled but not bulky, his slim hips, the back of his neck where his dark hair curls. He looks so unlike her husband, who's thick and muscled, covered everywhere with hair. Surely he can feel her gaze, but still he doesn't turn away from the sea.

"Why did you follow me out here?" she asks.

"I followed the scent of the ocean," he says.

"Stop lying."

He turns and smiles. His teeth are very white, and his cheeks dimple. For a moment he makes her think of Esme, although she doesn't know why.

"I followed you for the same reason all men follow you. I have designs upon your flesh."

"You still lie."

"Only partially."

Helen moves closer to him, near enough she has to look up to meet his eyes. She can feel his breath on her cheek, hot and smelling of wine and spices. She expects him to kiss her, or touch her. To take the invitation.

"Tell me your name," she says.

"Paris."

"The shepherd prince."

"So they call me."

She's heard about this young man, a prince of Troy, missing for years, raised by shepherds, only to reappear at the games, win all the contests, and then reveal his identity. She grips his forearms and can feel his muscles moving underneath his skin. She has a curious impulse to dig in her nails in order to get at whatever is underneath. She doesn't know why. She hasn't really wanted to touch a man since she was girl, just learning what her body did, what it made men think. When she was younger, before she was married, she used to flirt, and feel her own flesh thrill under the eyes of everyone who came to her father's palace. Her body used to make her feel powerful. She gives into her impulse and digs her nails in a little bit. He grimaces, but doesn't pull away.

"My husband calls me a snake," she says.

"I have a confession," he says.

She looks up into his eyes, and for a moment she feels as if she's looking into a strange sort of mirror, as though she's seeing her own eyes reflected in a male face. She's never met anyone else with eyes that look like hers, like the sky after a rain.

She asks him what he has to confess. After all, he's already admitted to lusting after another man's wife.

"Aphrodite gave you to me in exchange for a golden apple; I'm sorry," he says.

She drops her hands from his forearms. She sees that's she's made little half-moons on his skin that are now filling with blood. She turns and walks away without a word. She supposes she shouldn't be surprised, everyone always wants to exchange her for something. When Menelaus had her face stamped on a coin, she laughed, and he was hurt because he thought she'd be pleased. But really, she thought it was the most honest thing anyone had ever done for her. As she leaves Paris calls after her. He says that he's sorry, that he didn't know, that the gods are cruel and petty, and that he told her so she'd know the truth. He reminds her that she did order him to stop lying.

That night after the banquet Menelaus comes drunk to her bedroom. She's sitting, trying to play the lute. He pulls her to her feet and rips her dress down the front. He likes to do that, to destroy beautiful things. It makes him feel powerful and wealthy; he can destroy something valuable and then buy a replacement.

She tells him to slow down. Menelaus pulls off his own tunic. Helen thinks of Paris, of his dark hair, she wonders if her desire to touch him is only because of Aphrodite. She thinks of his slim, lithe body and tries not to look at Menelaus. Menelaus cups her breasts and rubs a rough thumb across her nipples. He thinks this is foreplay. She imagines Paris is touching her. She wonders if Menelaus would be gentler if she touched him back. She tries and he slaps her hand away, not hard, but a rejection all the same.

"Don't act like a whore," he says.

He told her once that his mother taught him that noble women, real women, don't like sex. She thinks his mother was a very unhelpful woman. She wonders what he does want, since she's cold one moment and whorish the next, according to him. He picks her up and drops her on the bed. Silently she dares him to notice the wound on her thigh, to ask her what's wrong. But instead he flips her over onto her stomach. She thinks of Esme, of how they'd tell each other stories into the night. When Esme helped her bathe and rubbed jasmine oil into her skin, she'd tell her she was beautiful, and Helen remembered how it felt to take some pride in that. Esme's hands were soft, not like Menelaus's, Menelaus pulls a bottle of olive oil from the table and rubs some on his hands, shoves his fingers inside her, then rubs himself with oil. Esme never hurt her. Esme saw her. Esme would have noticed the wound.

Afterwards Menelaus collapses next to her. The cut on her thigh broke open sometime during his rutting, and Helen can see little spots on the sheets. It reminds her of being a bride, the way the maids hung the bed sheet from the window. Menelaus's sweat smells sour. Helen curls up on her side, her knees pulled to her chest. Menelaus, uncharacteristically, hasn't left yet. She rolls onto to her other side and looks at him.

"What happened to Esme?" she asks.

She knows she might pay for the question, that he might laugh at her or taunt her with knowledge she doesn't want to know. But he won't strike her. At least he never does that. Menelaus turns towards her. He furrows his brow.

"Who?" he asks.

Helen feels like she's just stepped off one too many steps and stumbled—the ground retreating beneath her feet. He doesn't even remember Esme. He had her killed and forgot about her. Or perhaps Esme left on her own, ran away. No, that doesn't bear thinking about. Esme would never have left without a word. Besides, where else would she go? Her worries about Esme have been like a rotting tooth—she couldn't help but prod and poke. But Menelaus never even noticed. To Helen, the fact that Menelaus doesn't even remember Esme feels worse than if he had hit her.

"Just someone I knew," Helen says.

"Goodnight," he says, pats her shoulder, and stands up, wrapping a sheet around his hips. He leaves his discarded clothes on her floor.

The maid comes in and offers her a hot damp cloth. Helen cleans her cheeks and between her legs and the maid simply waits, silent, and then takes the cloth and leaves. Helen wraps herself in a robe and curls up in bed. No matter how many blankets she piles on she still wants more.

⁓

The next morning she sees Paris again at breakfast. He doesn't nod or smile; he just looks at her. His eyes seem to have changed color, grown more brilliant, like sapphires in his face. She has a hard time looking away. She feels as if there's a thread drawn between them, pulled taut, as if the Fates have both of them strung on their loom and are holding scissors poised. She tells herself not to imagine things. Menelaus sits next to her. He whispers in her ear, tells her thank you. Once again her looks have won the day. The ambassador wants to ally with them, and now all he has to do is convince the prince. His whiskers are rough. She turns her ear away from his lips. But she smiles at her husband, forms the shape of pleasure with her mouth, because she knows what she will say next.

"Would you like me to help you convince the prince? Take him for a walk by the shore?" she asks.

Menelaus, the fool, he thinks she can't possibly have any other motivations. He slaps her shoulder the way he would that of one of his soldiers.

"Yes, General Beauty, you do that."

She's been promoted from a snake to General Beauty. What rewards for volunteering. She swallows an acidic laugh. She bows her head gracefully, and picks up a small bowl of olives from the table in front of her. Cupping it in her hands she walks over to Paris. She can feel his eyes on her as she walks. She's suddenly very aware of her hips, of her waist, and the slight pain as her thighs brush the wound she made the day before. She stops in front of Paris and holds out the bowl of olives.

"These are my favorites," she says.

She watches his mouth as he takes an olive. She asks him to walk with her. She says she wants to show off the harbor, the excellent anchorage. She can hear Menelaus chortling at what he thinks is her outstanding innuendo. His voice comes as though from a distance. Paris stands up and motions for her to lead the way.

Down at the beach she takes off her sandals and wiggles her toes in the sand. Paris does the same.

"I was always barefoot when I watched the sheep," he says.

She pictures him as a shepherd, playing the lute, sitting in the sun on the grassy hills, all alone.

"Did it make you a poet?"

"A poor one, but yes."

She looks out at the waves. She imagines Esme's bones, tumbled in the sand, smoothed to pearls. Perhaps becoming the grain at the center of an oyster; the irritant that makes the beautiful, shining globe.

"Shall I call you the Shepherd Prince?"

"I'd prefer not."

He moves closer and picks up the long tail of her hair. He runs his fingers up to her scalp, loosens knots made by the wind, and he starts to braid her hair.

"I'll make you a warrior's knot," he says.

She asks him to tell her a story. So he does. He tells her how he used to sleep under the stars and watch the movements of the heavens. How he knows from the smell of the air when the flowers will start to bloom in the mountains. That once he saw a nymph frolicking in a stream. Whenever she dipped her limbs in the water they turned transparent, became the stream. The nymph saw him and invited him to swim. He lowered his eyes, and she told him that she wouldn't curse him; he was cursed enough already. As he braids Helen's hair, pulling her toward him until her head rests against his chest, she can feel the rise and fall of his breath. Then he tells her how his sister is a seer, how she says he'll bring the doom of Troy, how she won't look at him. He tells Helen how he misses the fields, how he misses being able to run and run until his breath can't enter his lungs fast enough. He longs for his shepherd family, and the way his shepherd mother used to sing as she worked. Yet he wants to be accepted and not called the Shepherd Prince; now he's not a shepherd, but not a real prince either. Not like his brother Hector, who is noble and good and strong, and uses a sword, a warrior's weapon. Not a bow like Paris.

"I think I'll forgive you," she says.

She means that she's decided to forgive him for winning her in a bet with the gods. The gods will have their way; her existence is a testament to that. And, he's nearly as Fate touched as she. She can feel it glowing off him.

He rubs his fingers in her scalp, over her neck and shoulders. He tells her that her hair must be heavy. She leans further back against him, his hips cupped against hers.

"I feel forgiven," he says.

"My running away with you will ruin the alliance. Your father, my husband, they'll both be furious," she says.

"But it will make me famous for daring, rather than for being a shepherd. What does a man have but his reputation?"

She hates this strange man's code, the idea that fame is the only thing that lasts, that great deeds are what matters. The longing for great deeds makes young boys go to war and come back broken. As the lady of the house she has to help stitch them up. The longing for fame made Menelaus purchase her from her family before he even met her. He wants his children to be grandchildren of Zeus. He wants to be able to say he fucks the divine (or half divine) every night. She's an accessory. Apparently Paris is not different from the rest of them.

"I don't know if I'll be able to love you," she says.

Paris traces a finger gently down her spine. He says he'll use his poet's ways. She can hear the smile in his voice. His hands have calluses, but he's gentle.

"I loved my maid, once," she says. She feels she must tell him, because of the echoes in his fingers.

"Sappho's my favorite poet," he says.

"I think Menelaus killed her."

The waves roll up. The tide begins to envelope their ankles. Still Paris lets her rest against his chest. He has an erection, but she doesn't blame him. Some things can't be helped.

"I don't really like killing. Men killing each other makes me feel sick," he says.

She understands that what he offers is a confession to balance hers, vulnerability for vulnerability. She likes him better for his un-warrior-like ways.

"I'll be your friend," he says.

The waves rush up to their knees, drenching her skirt, his tunic. She turns and looks him in the eyes, locks her hands behind his neck.

"Why do you want me?" she asks.

He kisses her softly on the lips. "Does it matter?"

She looks at him for a moment, and decides that it doesn't matter, really, why he wants her, because she thinks that probably he's the only person she's ever met who thrums in tune with her loneliness. He too exists between worlds. She thinks that perhaps the gods can move humans like goblets on a table, but they can't control the way the wine sloshes, spills. The small things, like her thoughts, her feelings, those things they can't see or hear.

"With tonight's tide," she says, stands up, and splashes through the water at a run.

Her muscles burn as she runs and the salt-water soaks her skin. When she sees Menelaus inside, he eyes her braided hair and her soaking wet clothes. She tells him that it's done, that she's made the alliance with Troy, which is true, but not in the way he thinks. She orders her maid to ready a bath. She goes all the way under water and opens her eyes, looking up at the world through the strange watery lens. She imagines she's the nymph from Paris's story, dissolving.

When the palace sleeps and the insects begin to sing to call back the dawn, Helen packs a bag with her clothes, with piles and piles of jewels. She doesn't feel like a thief. She just feels like she's taking what she's owed. So many times she's displayed herself for trade alliances and defense agreements. The wealth of Menelaus's small kingdom is at least partially due to her. She wraps herself in a black cloak and slips outside, barefoot to reduce sound. The halls seem cavernous, and it's hard to believe anyone ever lived here; it's as though the inhabitants are long dead and she walks through a ruin.

At the shore she sees a ship and Paris waiting in the sand. He too wears black. He tries to take her bag, to pick her up and carry her through the waves. She tells him no, says she'll walk herself. She does, and when the ambassador, looking displeased, reaches over the side of the boat and helps her up the ladder, she realizes she's grinning, that her cheeks are stretched with it. When Paris climbs up too, she runs to him and grabs his hand. She tells him to stand with her as they watch the shore disappear.

The ambassador says that he's a diplomat, not thief or kidnapper. But he mans the tiller anyway, because, well, he has to obey his prince. He repeats that he's not a thief.

Helen turns and looks at the ambassador. When she hears the fear in his voice, she knows that there will be consequences, blood on the waves, and yet she can't, won't, ask to be taken back.

"I steel myself," she says.

Jennifer Pullen received her BA from Whitworth University, her MFA from Eastern Washington University, and her PhD from Ohio University. She teaches at Ohio Northern University. Her poetry and fiction have appeared in journals and anthologies, including *Clockhouse*, *Prick of the Spindle*, *Phantom Drift Limited*, *Behind the Mask* (Meerkat Press), and *Lunch Ticket*. She grew up in the forests of Washington State and now lives in Northwestern Ohio with her husband and extremely demanding orange tabby.

A Bead of Amber on Her Tongue
by Jennifer Pullen

Cover art by Stephanie Law
"Awakened," watercolor. www.shadowscapes.com

Cover set in Adobe Garamond Pro
Interior set in Gramond 3 LT Std and Adobe Garmond Pro

Cover and Interior design by Trisha Peck

Printed in the United States
by Books International, Dulles, Virginia
On 55# Glatfelter B19 Antique
Acid Free Archival Quality Recycled Paper

Publication of this book was made possible in part by gifts from:
Mary Mackey, Francesca Bell, Katherine & John Gravendyk, in honor of Hillary
Gravendyk, and The New Place Fund

Omnidawn Publishing
Oakland, California
Staff and Volunteers, 2018–2019
Rusty Morrison & Ken Keegan, senior editors & co-publishers
Gillian Olivia Blythe Hamel, senior poetry editor & editor, OmniVerse
Trisha Peck, managing editor & program director
Cassandra Smith, poetry editor & book designer
Sharon Zetter, poetry editor and book designer
Liza Flum, poetry editor
Avren Keating, poetry editor & fiction editor
Juliana Paslay, fiction editor
Gail Aronson, fiction editor
SD Sumner, copyeditor
Emily Alexander, marketing manager
Lucy Burns, marketing assistant
Anna Morrison, marketing and editorial assistant
Terry A. Taplin, marketing assistant, social media
Caeden Dudley, editorial production assistant
Hiba Mohammadi, marketing assistant